# Seventy

LIANA BROOKS

# OTHER WORKS

Fey Lights
Prime Sensations


## HEROES AND VILLAINS

Even Villains Fall In Love
Even Villains Go To The Movies
Even Villains Have Interns
Even Villains Play The Hero (books 1 – 3 omnibus)


## TIME AND SHADOWS MYSTERIES

The Day Before
Convergence Point
Decoherence


## FLEET OF MALIK

Bodies In Motion
Change of Momentum
For Every Action (forthcoming)


Find other works by the author at
www.lianabrooks.com

# SEVENTY

INKLET #7

LIANA BROOKS

Inkprint PRESS

www.inkprintpress.com

Print ISBN: 978-1-925825-07-7
eBook ISBN: 9781386785811

www.inkprintpress.com

*National Library of Australia Cataloguing-in-Publication Data*
Liana Brooks 1982 –
Seventy
66 p.
ISBN: 978-1-925825-07-7
Inkprint Press, Canberra, Australia
1. Fiction—Short Stories 2. Fiction—Science Fiction 3. Fiction—Science Fiction—Space Exploration

First Print Edition: April 2019
Cover design © Inkprint Press
Interior art © Heather Craik

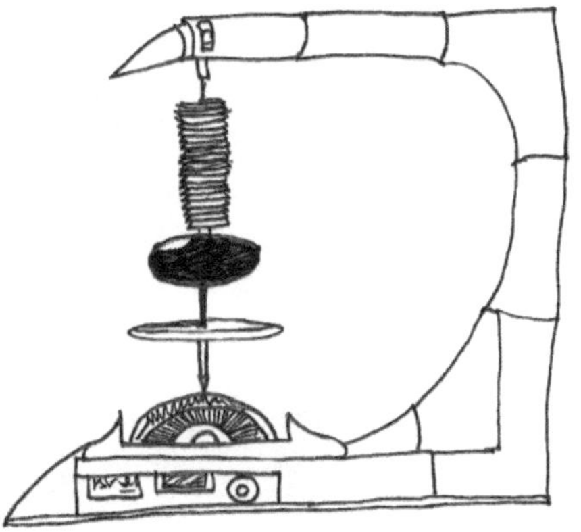

# SEVENTY

Oɴ ᴛʜᴇ ᴠɪᴇᴡ ꜱᴄʀᴇᴇɴ, ᴛʜᴇ Sᴏʟ Sʏꜱᴛᴇᴍ danced. Planets glowed like phosphorescent pearls in the sea of space. Doctor Jeff Koenig, lead scientist on the Dauphin settlement project, traced the image of Earth with his finger. He'd been born on Earth and left for the Delious system as soon as he could afford the emigration fees. Brilliant Delious, whose fourteen planets and all their many moons had been blasted into rubble by Hurluk world-destroyers. Only Delious Four remained, orbiting in isolation without her three moons.

He'd never meant to come back to Earth. Now he was leaving for a second time.

Earth had been too crowded when he'd left with his wife to start a new life out in the northern solar rim. Now the world-cities overflowed with refugees scattered by the Hurluk attacks. Accelerated terraforming on Dauphin wasn't the only plan to alleviate some of the housing pressure, but it was the only one that would show results within the next solar year.

Jeff frowned at the projection of Earth. How many of Sol's citizens really intended to emigrate to Dauphin?

Most people just wanted a place to abandon the refugees. But some would earn the money to buy their way free of the Sol system, and how many of those would come?

"Doctor Koenig?" Captain Mac of the *Terrance Lee* interrupted his reverie. "I need your crew to buckle down. We're hitting jump in twenty minutes."

"I thought everyone was settled." Jeff looked past the captain to the commons room where scientists mingled with the hired hands, all displaced workers paying back the cost of evacuation to the government. "Lawson."

"She's in the cargo bay."

Swearing, Jeff stalked down the hall. What had the congressional council been thinking when they assigned her to the team? But he knew the rumors; Doctor Bella Lawson threatened the wrong people, stepped on the wrong toes. So they'd dumped her on the Dauphin team.

If only he could dump her back.

She stood in an empty shuttle slot, staring at the bay door.

"Doctor Lawson?" Jeff said.

She pivoted, slowly.

"We need to strap down for jump."

Lawson pinned him with an angry glare, jaw clenched. "I'll be in my cabin."

He didn't bother arguing. All he needed to do was survive her tantrums for three months. Once Dauphin was open for settlement he'd move on, and she'd be back at Sol University driving someone else crazy with her conspiracy theories.

Captain Mac slapped Jeff's shoulder. "Mighty fine planet. I'm amazed what t-formers can do nowadays."

Both hands full of boxes, Jeff settled for a grimace and a nod. Dauphin was amazing: rolling green hills, majestic blue mountains, space enough for all of the refugees from Delious, Escibul, and the rest of the northern solar rim. "They've done a lot in thirteen months."

Mac cleared his throat. "I'm off. The first colonists are entering quarantine on Europa today. Seventy days, round trip. Will Dauphin be ready when we arrive?"

"The terraforming is finished, all my team needs to do is clear land for the living spires to drop, and make sure the crop rotations are started and ready to feed everyone." He could already see the green fields filling with the towering metal spikes embedded in black dirt. The self-contained towers would house homes and businesses—and act as temporary orbitals if the Hurluk turned Dauphin to dust under their feet.

"Living spires have hydroponics," Captain Mac said.

"Ground-grown foods are better for the body. Better for the spire's environmental system too. You can only push hydroponics so far."

"Doctor Koenig!" Shon Orto, Jeff's second-in-command and the coordinator for the first wave of science teams, shook papers over his head as he charged up the landing plateau.

Captain Mac shook his head. "Humans already? I don't understand why we risk personnel on a planet that's still terraforming. We have robots for a reason."

"Robots need maintenance. One circuit blows and all of a sudden your terraforming robot is thinking: 'I say, this planet would look so much more scenic with some volcanoes all over the place'." Jeff shuddered. He looked at Shon. "How are things?"

"Interesting. I just got some new readings in."

"Right." Jeff handed Shon a box of basic vaccines and smiled at Captain Mac. "No rest for the weary."

"See you in a few months." The captain waved and walked back to his shuttle.

Shon shoved papers at Jeff. "We're having some trouble with the third continent's major fault line."

Jeff sighed. "That's just the kind of news I don't want to hear."

By nightfall, when Jeff stumbled to his makeshift room in the main building, the *Terrance Lee* was a green blip entering the wormhole for her return to the Sol System.

He was stranded a galaxy away from home with five hundred strangers on an unstable planet.

Seventy days. He was only stranded for seventy days, then things would be well once again.

"You idiot!" Bella Lawson raged at Shon Orto, spinning her chair away from the computer screen. "You should have loaded everyone back on the *Terrance Lee* the moment we touched down."

Jeff shook his head. "Doctor Lawson, I don't think—"

"I'm not surprised," she snarled at him. Lawson turned back to Shon. "The SOP for earthquakes on a t-forming planet is to evacuate until stabilization is confirmed."

"Time is not a luxury we have," Shon said. "We have contracts. We have to—"

"You won't do anything if you're dead." Lawson slammed down the readouts. "I can't believe anyone signed off on this planet. I told Congress we couldn't move forward with the SHORTMIN t-forming. It isn't safe. But a well-placed bribe speaks louder than facts."

The last thing Jeff wanted was to give Lawson a chance to rave about a corrupt Congress endangering colonization. He cleared his throat. "Sol System can't absorb more refugees. The ones from Delious have no choice, they don't have planets left to live on. But with the natives from Escibul pouring in as well, humanity needs room to expand. If people weren't convinced that the Hurluk are headed for them next, it wouldn't be so bad."

Lawson rolled her eyes. "There's no evidence to suggest the Hurluk will move to Echo Territory next. They can't use our wormhole technology. From the Delios System they have dozens of star systems to invade. If you want to suggest they'll move their planet-destroyers in a straight line you might as well evacuate the Sol System too. They're next in line after Escibul."

She took a deep breath and looked at the printouts again, then shook her head. "We need to evacuate. The data doesn't lie."

"We can't." Jeff held up a placating hand. "I agree, it's the standard operating procedure. But where are we going to go? There's no other habitable planet in system. We have no orbiting base. And we can't live in shuttles for the next three months."

Shon raised his hand. "Maybe you're overreacting? Dauphin was signed off on. The original t-form expert considered the planet stable. What are the other possibilities?"

With a frustrated sigh, Lawson looked back at the seismograph.

"Could this be part of the natural settling process?" Jeff prompted.

"Possibly." Lawson pursed her lips. "If Doctor Orto"—she cut a glare at Shon—"hadn't been drilling, it's possible the tremors would have gone unnoticed. I can't guarantee anything though."

"We're not asking you to." Shon threw his hands up in the air. "Look, just tell me how to fix it."

"Fix it?" She laughed. "You can't 'fix' a shaking planet, Doctor Orto. There's nothing to fix. This is part of the process. If you like, I can tell you exactly what's happening and why. Or what will happen next. But I can't undo this."

"Then what good are you?"

"Shon?" Angeliessa Sahn, the horticulturist, walked in smiling. Her expression froze when she saw Bella's hard glare. "I—I just needed to talk to Doctor Orto."

"We're having a private conference," Lawson said coldly.

"Shon, there's nothing more you can do here. Go see what Miss Sahn needs." Jeff watched Shon chase eagerly after the pretty blonde. Well, best of luck to him.

Jeff turned back to the t-form expert. "Give me facts. What are we dealing with?"

"SHORTMIN cuts the standard terraforming time from six years plus colonization to ten months by cutting out two of the three ice age stages. All the glacial carving and continent sorting is done in six weeks."

"I know that. Tell me what this means." He stabbed the readout.

"I think it means we're entering third stage t-forming. Another ice age. This could be sixth stage settling, but I doubt it. Either way, we won't know until something drastic happens, or doesn't. SHORTMIN was never tested on a large planet. Dauphin is the lab rat. We shouldn't be here."

He was getting tired of the repetition. "We don't have a choice." Jeff stared at the readouts as though wishing would change them. He sighed. "I hope you're wrong."

"Dr. Koenig," she said, "if I was wrong on a regular basis, they'd have had no need to ship me off-world."

"I get germination in four hours and maturation in a week. Each plant produces enough for six people for the three weeks it fruits. I'm trying to push the next generation to fruiting in five days with a four week growing season—"

Lawson walked into the greenhouse, knocking aside a row of pots in her hurry. "Doctor Koenig, I need to speak to you."

"This is a private conference!" Angeliessa snapped, moving to right the pots.

Jeff sighed, aware that he was caught in the cross-fire of the first civil war on Dauphin. "Can it wait thirty minutes?"

"No."

"Fine." He smiled at Angeliessa. "Excuse me, I'll be right back." Jeff followed Lawson out of the greenhouse and across the lawn towards the gray, rectangular monstrosity that was both HQ and housing. "What's going on?"

She shoved a piece of paper at him.

Jeff frowned at the jumping line on the paper. "Readouts from the drill probes? I thought you said it was something important."

"This is new. It's the readings from a seismograph on continent five."

"It's gibberish to me." He handed the read-out back.

She pointed to a spike that touched the top of the chart. "That's a major upheaval event."

"Are you sure?"

She gave him a withering look. "No. Maybe it was a butterfly jumping on the sensor? Of course I'm sure!"

"What do you want me to do?"

"Authorize a survey team to go to the fifth continent to check for visual confirmation, and assess damage."

Jeff watched Doctor Lawson's shuttle appear over the horizon, a black speck against the waning afternoon light, then refocused on what Shon was saying. "I'm sorry, repeat that, how much land is cleared?"

"Enough for the first four hundred spires. Bare minimum, that's four thousand people."

"We won't see spires with less than two thousand colonists," Jeff said. "Not with the news outlets running images of the Hurluk attacks night and day."

"Right." Shon scribbled on his pad. "I don't think we need to worry about that. My only concern is the native flora. It's the t-weed—fast-growing, adaptable, annoying at this stage. We needed it to produce the oxygen during t-forming, but it's going to clog the oxygen intake vents on the spires.

I recommend a controlled burn followed by reseeding with a slower growing plant."

"Fine. Do you have the next section selected for clearing?"

"The north plateau. I just need Doctor Lawson to sign off on it."

"I'll send her over once she reports in." Jeff scrubbed his hands through his hair. Today wasn't the worst day they'd had, but he certainly hoped Doctor Lawson bore good news.

The shuttle blew up dark dust as it settled. There was a soft "whump" as the anti-grav turned off and the ship dropped the last centimeter to the ground.

Jeff waited.

The doors cycled open and the survey crew exited, carrying a battered seismograph. Lawson followed, red-eyed and shaking.

"We need to evacuate. Now."

"What?"

"It's all gone. Fifth continent's been swallowed by a volcano. There's nothing but ash and lava, it's the size of Olympus Mons on Mars. We can't stay."

"We can't go! Do you want to sit on a shuttle for the next two months?"

"Yes!" Her breath stuttered as she sucked in air. "SOP—"

"SOP be hanged! We'll die of carbon monoxide poisoning on the shuttles. They aren't meant for long-term use. This continent is stable? Isn't it?"

She bit her lip. "Temporarily. This is Third Stage t-forming. Our weather patterns—"

"Will change. We might get cold. But it won't kill us in the next sixty days," Jeff said firmly.

"We have to adjust the genetics of

the crops. The ash is going to cause a volcanic winter." She looked at him, eyes cold as the winter she was predicting. "Doctor Koenig, if things get worse, if the tremors hit us here, we *need* to evacuate."

Jeff shook his head. "We'll weather this, Bella. We have do."

Somehow. Somehow they would find a way.

Glass shattered. His bed jumped, screeching as it shimmied across the floor. Jeff rolled, landing hard on his knees, and scrambled to the shelter of his doorway. "Lawson?"

Something fell in her office, but no one answered.

"Shon?" Jeff pushed himself to his feet. He shook as he opened the blackout curtain. Pale pink moonlight streamed in on the wreckage of his study. Grabbing a flashlight, he checked Lawson's office first. She wasn't there.

How much would Congress fine him for losing a t-form specialist?

Aftershocks rocked the ground. Jeff stumbled, throwing an arm out for balance. "Lawson? Shon? Where are you?"

Fire backlit the skeleton of the wooden barn. A soot-covered Shon ran up to meet him. "What is this?" Shon said. "I was checking the barn before I went to bed and…" He waved his hand at the chaos.

The barn was burning—Jeff made a mental note to find out who hadn't secured the flammables in the appropriate locker—part of the shuttle bay roof had collapsed, and the greenhouse had been reduced to slivers of glass.

"Why didn't we get a warning?" Shon looked around in confusion. "Where is Angeliessa?"

Jeff glared at him as the ground shuddered. "How should I know? Where is Lawson? She's the one responsible for tracking these things."

Shon pointed across to the shuttle bays. "Shouting at someone."

"Go round up the science staff, we're meeting in ten minutes."

Jeff pushed tables aside to make space for the meeting in the cafeteria. Outside, workers shouted as they tried to corral the animals and put out the fire.

"Is this the meeting place?" A short, balding man with a wiry build shuffled into the room, laden with paperwork.

Jeff didn't recognize him. He set the last chair in place and frowned. "I'm Doctor Koenig, the project director. Who are you?"

"Doctor Berrans." The little man didn't offer a hand. He dropped his papers on the table and smirked. "I'm actually here with the EPP."

The broad smile only made Jeff want to punch him. "The what?"

"Energy Planet Program. Orator Rens pushed it through Congress a few months ago. Very important. Cutting edge. Turn the entire inner planet, the unnamed rock spiralling into the sun, into an energy source."

His fists clenched. "Isn't that a considerable waste of resources? We'll lose everything we put there when the planet falls into the sun."

"That won't happen for centuries," Berrans said. "Considering all the information we'll gain from our science stations the waste is negligible."

"Never mind." Jeff shook his head. "Why didn't you introduce yourself when I arrived?"

"Why would I have?" Doctor Berrans asked in surprise. "I'm the senior project director. Not that I would comment on your lack of introduction, I realize most of the personnel are working on your project. But since I arrived first—"

"You weren't supposed to be here at all! The EPP was scheduled to start with the fourth wave of colonists."

Doctor Berrans waved his hand. "The sooner I start, the sooner we have the energy sump."

"Right now we need a way to get off Dauphin and survive until Captain Mac comes back." Jeff looked at the rest of the frowning science staff: Shon, Angeliessa, Lawson… "Where's the shuttle rep, and Doctor Keeler?"

"Keeler is corralling the animals with his workers," Shon said. "He told me to tell you he doesn't care what happens as long as we promise not to destroy anything else. Marcus is still at the shuttle bay assessing damage."

"We'll start without them." Jeff turned to glare at Lawson. "Why weren't we warned this was coming?"

"Because we have no sensor grid system or seismograph in our area," she said with cold calm.

Jeff swore.

"What's happening to Dauphin?" Angeliessa asked. "I put out the cold-tolerant crops like Doctor Lawson ordered. But I don't have crops engine-eered to handle earthquakes."

"Dauphin is entering Third Stage terra-forming," Lawson said.

"Which is what?" Angeliessa asked.

"Earthquakes, upheaval events, drastic changes in topography, and it ends with a cataclysmic ice age." Lawson folded her arms across her chest.

An ELE, an extinction-level event. The thought made Jeff's blood run cold. "This isn't Third Stage. SHORT-MIN drops the t-forming process from five stages to three, and the ELE you're describing has already happened on Dauphin. This is something else."

"The tests for SHORTMIN were performed on asteroids and moons much smaller than Dauphin. I don't think the forced thaw of the ice age that ends the Third Stage was enough to lock the tectonic plates." Lawson paused, then set her lips in a thin line. "We need to evacuate."

"Maybe things will settle down," Angeliessa protested. "Normal planets have 'quakes, don't they?"

Lawson glanced at Jeff. "I've been tracking the tremors on the other continents. They're increasing in frequency and intensity. The new volcano on the fifth continent is primed to erupt again. We're already seeing the ash in the air. It's only going to get worse."

"Where do we go?" Shon asked. "What was the plan for this?"

"We move to the orbital support," Doctor Berrans said. The grating smile reappeared. "SOP."

Jeff glared at the obnoxious man. "We don't have orbital support. The Congressional Space Fleet is helping with evacuation of Escibul. The orators didn't think a ship could be spared for orbital support when the planet was stable and habitable."

"Idiots," Lawson hissed.

"That's not lawful!" Berrans sputtered. "I must file a complaint. Orator Rens will hear about this."

"What do we do?" Shon asked, reaching for Angeliessa's hand.

"We evacuate on the shuttles and hope we can hold off until the *Terrance Lee* arrives in system. Maybe do a slow burn towards the wormhole," Jeff said. "What else could we do?"

Doctor Berrans raised his hand.

Jeff gave him a cold look. "Yes?"

"On the spiral planet we have a research station. Nineteen burrowing drones to act as housing and room for hydroponics. The atmosphere is rich in oxygen. If Miss Sahn"—he nodded curtly at Angeliessa—"will work on hydroponics, we can stay there for several weeks."

"What happens after several weeks?" Shon asked.

Doctor Berrans sneered. "We run out of water, obviously. That close to the sun no water would stay in a liquid state for long."

"I vote for the shuttles," Lawson said.

"We'll suffocate," Berrans argued.

"We can adjust for respiration rates; we can't cut water rations."

"I need a few weeks to fix the shuttle's hydroponics and add algae tanks to purify the air," Angeliessa said.

"We don't have that kind of time." Lawson shook her head. "You'll have to do that in orbit."

Jeff stood. "We'll go to the spiral planet, regroup, outfit the shuttles, and leave for the wormhole. I want the first group evacuating in three days."

The long-range scanner, meant to warn the colony if Hurluks came, sat silent in the corner. Jeff tapped his pen on the empty desktop, staring at the blank screen as if will alone could make the *Terrance Lee* appear. Thirty-four days, just keep them all safe for thirty-four days.

Shon Orto knocked on the door and let himself in. "We've got a problem."

Jeff sighed, rocking his chair back. "Another one?"

"We have nine shuttles, each with an optimal load of thirty people."

"Angeliessa's algae tanks will give us enough oxygen for the rest. We only have just over four hundred people on planet—"

Shon's face turned stoic. "Four hundred ninety-seven."

Jeff shook his head. "No we don't, we have—"

"Doctor Berrans' team wasn't part of the count."

"We only have nine shuttles." Jeff swore. "That was one less than I requisitioned. Didn't Berrans get any?"

"He signed for five," Shon said. "Which would have covered his team and their equipment—"

"But someone in Congress decided we didn't really need those shuttles," Jeff finished for him. "I want to think our shuttles are helping the evacuation effort, not ferrying some lobbyist around."

Shon grimaced. "We could dream. But it still doesn't give us the room. As it is, we have seven shuttles total. One is scrap, the other won't be space worthy without major repairs. Anyway I set this up, we can't take everyone. Some-one has to stay."

"Not on Dauphin. We'll go to the spiral planet." Jeff made a mental note to name the place when they got there.

"And then we'll sort it out. Maybe we can find a way to extend our survival time there."

Cold wind whipped ash into drifts along the edge of buildings, covering everything in a fine layer of grit. Another volcano had erupted while they slept, this one closer to the valley. It was only a matter of time before the little home they'd built was devoured by lava.

He went to the empty office, staring at the blank wall, wishing desperately for a drink to drown reality for a few hours.

"Jeff?" Lawson slipped in, shutting the door behind her. "The first shuttle is ready to go. Why aren't you on it?"

"I'm the project lead. I need to make sure everyone gets off safe. "

"This shuttle is getting away. I'm not sure that next one will. Your family will want to see you again..."

She was supposed to be shipping out on that shuttle; she wanted to put him there instead. For the first time since the earthquakes started, he smiled. "My family's dead, Bella. They were on Delious Seven when it was destroyed. I was on Delious Four, attending a conference. If I'd taken them with me…"

Lawson hesitated, then a faint blush dusted her cheeks. "I met you there. When my ex-fiancé came to yell at me, you stepped in."

Jeff blinked. He vaguely recalled a thin, dark-haired woman, and a drunk. "It's been a long time. You two never got back together?"

"No. I wanted something he couldn't offer." Her smile turned bitter. "It's ancient history. And you don't have time to talk."

"Send this instead." Jeff patted the long-range scanner. "Seeing Captain Mac arrive early will do more for morale than I can."

The skulking gray hulk of Dauphin fell away. Beautiful, hope-filled, Dauphin. Dreams turned to dust.

Bella slipped her hand into his and squeezed. "I'm sorry."

"So am I."

Kicks were the only language the power converter understood. Jeff started each day by communicating forcefully with the machine. To stop the cold air from turning his testicles to icicles while he slept, he had to kick the thing again in the evening.

"Jeff?" Shon Orto walked in wearing a sweat-soaked undershirt and regulation pants cut to the knees.

"It's working again."

"Good. Berrans is on the radio."

He twisted his neck, working out a crick. "About time we got those things up and running." Jeff took over the radio, the only way to communicate when daylight temperatures made leaving the buried buildings a death sentence. "Koenig here."

"I found a way to extend our water supply," Berrans said.

"How long?"

"Months. Dauphin was dry when it was t-formed. The water was brought in from ice rings around the third planet. We could fill a shuttle and bring it in. We could even use the broken shuttle as an ice mule, just tug it along behind. The ice won't need oxygen or gravity."

"Do we have the fuel for that?"

"As much as we could ever want. The shuttles use charged solar cells."

And sunlight was not something cloudless Spiral was lacking. "Contact the pilots. I'm dying for a real bath."

Jeff ran a manual check on the long-range radar, pinging the distant probes, waiting for the reply. The probes responded. The endless night of space stayed empty.

"Shon?" Jeff walked into the living area. Quarters were cramped, for now, but they were surviving.

The younger man looked up from the table where he was playing a scratch game of checkers with his new wife. "Any news?"

"Can we get one of the shuttles to check their long-range?"

"Still no Captain Mac?"

"I'm seeing nothing."

"He might be delayed," Angeliessa said. "Maybe loading took longer than planned."

"Probably." Jeff forced a smile. He left the common room to hide in his own small apartment, not willing to voice his secret fear. The Hurluk only needed to go in a straight line from Escibul to Earth.

"The only thing we can do is send a shuttle to the Sol System for a ship," someone argued over the radio. Jeff had lost track of the argument thirty minutes ago. They'd gone from constructive ideas to hysteria in record time.

Shon leaned over and hit the com button. "The stresses of re-entry into real space will rip the hull apart. You'll be shrapnel on the edge of inhabited space."

"Staying here is death!" another man screamed. "We have to leave before this planet hits the sun. How many years do we have before the heat broils us alive in these tombs?"

"Hundreds of years," Berrans said.

Jeff took the radio to stop the shouting match. "This isn't death. It just isn't a good life. This is sustainable, and until a larger vessel arrives to rescue us the only thing we can do is concentrate on sustaining life. Someone will find us before Spiral reaches a critical orbit."

He shut the radio off and covered his eyes before anyone could say, "Hurluk."

"Someone's going to try and take a shuttle," Shon said.

"There's no way to stop them," Jeff answered.

Sitting beside Shon, Angeliessa rubbed her growing belly. "If we re-organized the housing, that might make people less antsy. Everyone was tossed together at random. If we had more couples…"

Jeff nodded. It might be just enough to keep people sane. And trying it was better than doing nothing.

Shuttle Four cruised across the radar screen, an insignificant green speck representing twenty-seven desperate lives.

Bella pushed the curtain to Jeff's living area aside. "Aren't you coming out? Dauphin is rising against the moons. It's almost pretty, from here."

"What does the surface look like?"

"Red and boiling." She tugged at his hand, a playful smile on her lips. "Come on. We all need fresh air. We only have an hour before the temperatures get too low. Watching the screen won't change anything."

He bit his lip. Bella leaned closer. Jeff gave in. "I'm coming."

Prying the back panel off the long-range scanner, Jeff scrounged for wires to fix the cooling unit. He tore three short wires out and put the panel back before pushing the scanner into the corner. Space was at a premium, especially with a baby on the way.

He wrapped his knuckles one more time on the scanner, trying to remember the old terror of abandonment, the nightmares that gave him sleepless nights when they'd first arrived.

But it was gone now, joining Dauphin and Earth in the world of distant dreams. Myths. Bedtime stories for tired children.

He gave the converter a warning kick as he walked back to the kitchen. Dinner was almost ready.

# THE MAKING OF
## *SEVENTY*

This was originally part of an anthology call. They wanted exploration of new planets, I had to find the backstory for *Red Planet Refugees*, and somehow this is what happened.

The story never made it to the anthology, but it was my first published short story, in an e-zine that went defunct in 2013. It's been printed, reprinted, and here it is again: the story about scientists who have seventy days to live.

# Read more by Liana Brooks!

# PRIME SENSATIONS

"Unidentified vessel, we are Waste Hauler 133 out of Darrian 6. We carry no trade or crew," the ship's AI droned in a bored monotone.

Lana dropped into the waste hauler's modified control booth and took over. "Unidentified vessel, be advised. I steer like a drunken moose, alter your course." The reverb over the frequently patched comm lines made her sound like an old man with a lifelong bitter-root habit.

Sweat dripped down her nose. The waste hauler had a hull thirty years older than she was, and an environmental system older than that. It had survived two major system wars by being too worthless to target. And Lana was well aware that, as a debtor working off her ransom to the Iloni nation, she was slightly less valuable than the ship.

The comm crackled and she thought she heard the word "boarding."

"Unidentified vessel," she replied, "I am deaf and blind. I give you no authorization to come near this vessel. If you keep to your projected course I will have no choice but to heartlessly smash your hull because of physics."

The other ship tried to respond.

Lana grimaced and tried to compensate for the ancient communications array. "Mass times acceleration, unidentified vessel. I can't slow down in time."

"Waste Hauler 133, this is the *Marsail* out of Port Tael, flying the flag of the Exaner Confederation. Prepare to be boarded."

Black holes and dark nights! Port Tael was a pirate station, taken by the outer rim unification during the Apex

War, and currently under stars only knew which warlord.

She leaned against the rough metal of the control booth. They probably wanted to pick over the hauler for parts. Stars knew there was enough wreckage welded in to rebuild a fleet. She should probably get dressed.

Lana sniffed her armpit. Maybe a shower was in order. And clothes. And snacks. The *Marsail* wouldn't cross paths with her hauler for a few more hours, and it was the most exciting thing to happen since she'd been taken as a prisoner of war three years ago.

A shower and change of clothes later, Lana watched as the *Marsail* managed to land on the bulky waste hauler with a finesse Lana would have envied a few years ago, back when she'd thought her rift rat piloting skills would be enough to win the attention she craved.

It never had.

She tossed a boiled nut into her mouth and watched the pirate crew's slow progress through the hull. If there'd been someone to bet against, she would have wagered they'd go for the hard metals compartment, maybe grab some radiated shielding or a new engine converter.

Her second bet was the food waste department, where they might try panning for seeds. Not that it would do them any good—the Iloni poisoned the food waste to ensure the vegetation of Darrian 6 wasn't sold on the black market—but they were welcome to try.

The enemy ship latched on like a leech and sliced through her hull. The crew moved methodically toward the control deck.

If she'd had a weapon, she would have gone out to meet them. The only gear worth having was the bits she'd salvaged. Not enough to build a shuttle, not yet, but in another year or three she'd have a means of escape. If they took that...

Lana eyed the console and considered the maneuvers she'd need to shake the smaller ship off. Scraping them against the mine corridor that kept her from diverting off course sounded promising.

She was running over the possible course corrections needed when someone banged on the door of the control booth.

"Pilot?" The person hammered on the door again. "Waste Hauler Pilot, open this door."

She raised an eyebrow and grabbed another boiled nut. Telling the intruder she'd survived far worse than they could dish out was a waste of oxygen. Right now, she was breathing. If that changed in the next few minutes, no one was going to care, least of all her.

"Open this door or we will open it for you."

"Be my guest."

"Stand back."

She looked around at the cramped booth, a cylinder of buttons, viewing screens, and control panels. Given enough time and the right tools, she could rip out the main radar and stuff herself into the box, but that would take at least an hour.

The door in front of her radiated heat.

Lana lifted the chair that had long ago rusted loose just in time to prevent hot metal shrapnel from hitting her face.

"Hi." She set the chair down so she could look into the black faceplate of her attacker. With a smile, she slapped the panic button that sent the waste hauler into a death spiral, alarm beacons screaming. "Iloni forces will be here within the hour. Do you want to shoot me now, or later?" The increased gravity of the spiral pulled at her. For a moment it looked like her attacker planned on retreating. She winked at the black face mask. "Pretty girl got your tongue?"

The invader pushed past her, boots scraping along the floor, and fumbled to hit the bypass code with large hands. "You think I don't know that trick?"

"You think I care what you know?"

The faceplate cleared as he turned to her. And Lana found herself staring into the shocked eyes of Kaleb Hath—the man who'd left her for dead.

Lana's nails bit into her palms as her fists clenched. "Commander Hath," she said, "if I'd known it was you, I would have vented my oxygen an hour ago."

Keep reading! Head to:
http://www.lianabrooks.com/books/short-stories/
to buy your copy now!

# ABOUT THE AUTHOR

LIANA BROOKS has never been off her home planet, but she hopes that one day NASA will call her up and offer her the job as writer-in-residence for any mission going anywhere. It sounds like fun.

Until that happy day, she can be found busily inventing new worlds for science fiction fans to explore in her study in the Pacific Northwest.

She has written the popular *Time and Shadows Mysteries* series about clones and the dangers of time travel; the *Fleet of Malik* series of connected sci-fi romances about re-building after a decades long war; and the cult-following *Heroes and Villains* series of superhero romances.

You can find out more about Liana at her website, www.lianabrooks.com.

SEVENTY
LIANA BROOKS

A Final Request for Mercy
AMY LAURENS

the kitten psychologist
vs.
the kitten's owners
THEA VAN DIEPEN

Answer the Question
AMY LAURENS

Happily, Red
AMY LAURENS

the kitten psychologist
tries to be patient
through email
THEA VAN DIEPEN

RED PLANET
REFUGEES
LIANA BROOKS

the kitten psychologist &
What The Kitten Did
THEA VAN DIEPEN

INKLET #018
Cherry
Blossom
AMY LAURENS

Alone
AMY LAURENS

the kitten psychologist
& The Kitten
Come To A Conclusion
THEA VAN DIEPEN

LEVEL NINE
LIANA BROOKS

INKLET #020
To Dust
AMY LAURENS

INKLET #021
Interchange
AMY LAURENS

INKLET #022
Emalia's
Lanterns
LIANA BROOKS

INKLET #023
Dear Santa
AMY LAURENS

INKLET #024
The
Quilt-Maker's
Scrap
AMY L. LAURENS

www.ingramcontent.com/pod-product-compliance
Lightning Source LLC
Chambersburg PA
CBHW031035190726
48286CB00003BA/1185